It's Christmas!

Tracey Corderoy

Tim Warnes

dinosaurs
bricks
sledge!
digger

LITTLE TIGER
LONDON

Christmas was coming
and Archie was excited.
More excited than **EVER!**

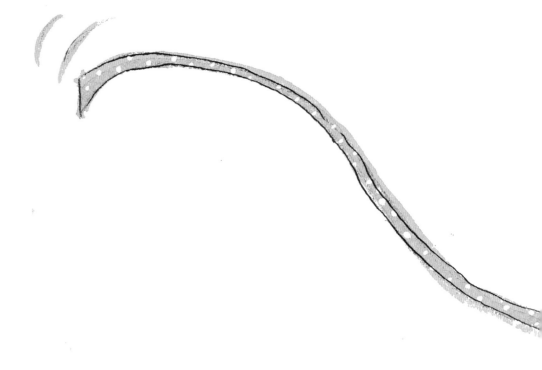

Dad's Christmas biscuits smelled yummy.

But Archie wanted to make them
even better.

So he plopped on more icing and shook on **LOTS** of sprinkles.

"Look, Dad!" said Archie.
"Christmas penguins!"

Next Archie helped Mum decorate the tree. But the new decorations weren't quite right . . .

So Archie found the old ones instead.

He even found the star
that **NEVER** stopped flashing!
"Now it really feels like Christmas!"
Archie smiled.

Ding-dong! went the doorbell.
It was Granny and Grandpa in their lovely
Christmas jumpers!

Archie looked
down at his
jumper and
sighed.

It's not
Christmassy
enough!

So out came his craft box and Archie got busy . . .

"Ta-daa!" Archie beamed, and he gave a little twirl.

"Mind the tree!" Grandpa cried as it

wibbled and **wobbled** and . . .

"Now then," said Mum, "I wonder . . .
who would like a **VERY** Christmassy job?"

Mum sat Archie down by the window.
"I need you to watch . . . for snow,"
she whispered.

"Yay!" cheered Archie.
"Snow is **SUPER**-Christmassy!"

Archie waited, and **waited**, and **WAITED**.

But the snow didn't come.

Not

one

flake.

This isn't Christmassy at **ALL!**

Even Tiger looked sad.

But then Archie had a brilliant idea . . .

"Oh, Archie!" sighed Dad. "Look – you've buried all the presents in the snow!"

So Archie swept the snow off the presents.
But – **OOPS!** – he swept the labels off too!

Where did each one GO?

By Christmas morning everything felt perfectly Christmassy – there was even REAL snow!

"Time to open some presents!" Mum called. They all gathered round. But – **oh dear** – something wasn't quite right.

Dad had Granny's balls of wool,
Mum had Grandpa's fishing rod,
Granny had Dad's drum kit,
and Archie had Mum's
favourite perfume!

Then Grandpa opened the best present of all . . .

Luckily, Mum put everything right.

But Granny loved Dad's drums so much, they let her bang out one more Christmas carol. Now even Archie had to agree . . .

This was the most
Christmassy Christmas **EVER!**